To my buddy Greyson: You're the bee's knees.

Library of Congress Cataloging-in-Publication Data:

Nichols, Travis, author.
Fowl play / by Travis Nichols.
pages cm.
Summary: A team of animal sleuths is hired to solve the mystery of a broken window.
ISBN 978-1-4521-3182-5 (alk. paper)
1. Animals—Juvenile fiction. 2. Humorous stories. [1. Mystery and detective stories. 2. English language—Idioms—Fiction. 3. Animals—Fiction. 4. Humorous stories.] I. Title.

PZ7.N544Fo 2015
[E]—dc23

2014024307

Manufactured in China.

Design by Ryan Hayes.
Lettering by Travis Nichols.
The illustrations in this book were rendered in pencil on paper and colored digitally.

10 9 8 7 6 5 4 3 2 1

Chronicle Books LLC
680 Second Street
San Francisco, California 94107

Chronicle Books—we see things differently. Become part of our community at www.chroniclekids.com.

FOWL PLAY
Travis Nichols
chronicle books · san francisco
Looks like another dull as dishwater day.
ALERT

ALERT

GUMSHOE ZOO! In a pickle?

Hello, detective agency? This is Mr. Hound.
GUMSHOE ZOO
DETECTIVE AGENCY
63-6802

GUMSHOE ZOO
DETECTIVE AGENCY
63-680

I need your help.

Mike
You've got your goat, sir. We're on the case!
Josie
BEEP
BEEP
ALERT
Sharon
Antoine

All right, team. Opportunity knocks!
Reggie
Steve
Morgan
Quentin
Four... five... six...
GUMSHOE ZOO

Thanks for coming, detectives. Someone broke my store window last night.

We'll take it from here, Mr. Hound.
Hmm... Yes. There's something fishy going on around here.

Oh! No offense, Reggie.
None taken.

But you are right.

window:
-glass
-broken

There is some definite monkey business at hand, my friend.

Ooh. I didn't mean anything by that, Steve.
No sweat.
ENTER

And I agree. I smell a rat.

Yikes! Sorry, Josie.
I understand.

I, too, suspect foul play.

Oh! Morgan! I apologize.

No need, Josie. That was F-O-U-L. I'm a chicken. That's F-O-W-L.

Now let's grab the bull by the horns and solve this case!

Hey!

Sorry about that. I just thought...

It's cool. Water off a duck's back.

Oops! Sharon. I am SO sorry.
Don't mention it, buddy.

Hold it.

I don't think I'm barking up the wrong tree here. Whoops... sorry, Mr. Hound.

Sure sure sure. Um... hey... I think there's some... um... evidence... away from here.

Look! A mistake in the lettering!

So what?

So maybe you saw the mistake on your window, but you didn't want to pay an arm and a leg to fix it.
Mr. Hound's
Grociries
open 7-7 M-F

So you cooked up a scheme to break it ...

... and called us so you could get it fixed for free.

A-HA! That's IT, isn't it?
What's the matter? Cat got your tongue?

Hold your horses! I won't be your scapegoat!

HOW DARE YOU!

You're all canned! Beat it!

No, YOU'RE the one who's canned.
You're under arrest.

It's time to face the music.

You gotta reap what you sow.

It's the price you have to pay.

The chickens have come home to roost.

Sorry, Morgan.

It's fine. Let's just wrap this up.

Take him to the big house, officers.
Way to use your noodle, Sharon!

Yes, the sky's the limit for—what's that?

We interrupt this story to bring you an urgent report of a situation developing downtown.
W-IDM 4

Get those detectives over here. On the double.
It's a... jumbo... shrimp.
MAYOR

The idiom-tastic case of the broken window was a breeze, but will our favorite sleuths be able to solve the mystery behind this beast of oxymoronic proportions?
STAY TUNED!

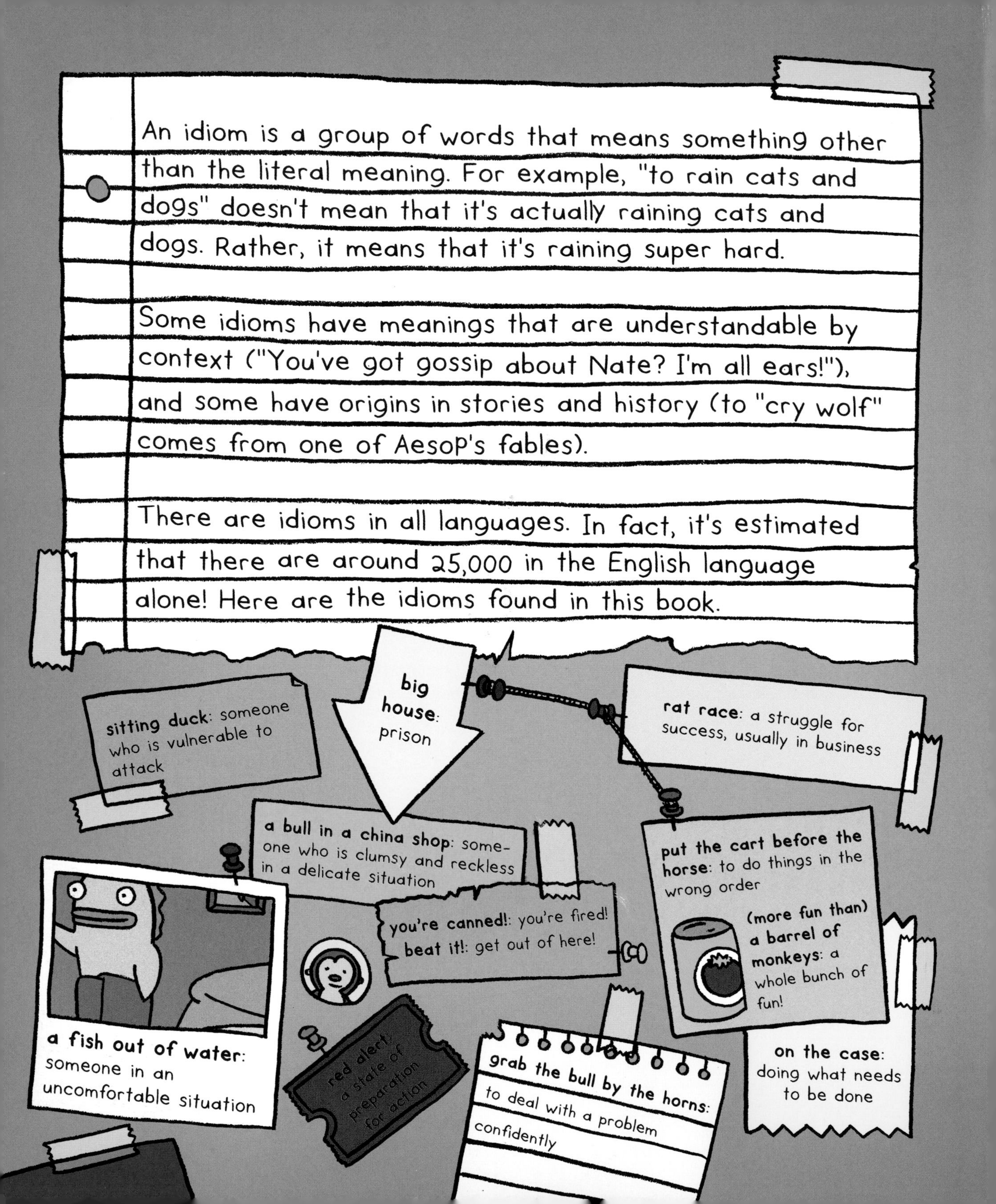
An idiom is a group of words that means something other than the literal meaning. For example, "to rain cats and dogs" doesn't mean that it's actually raining cats and dogs. Rather, it means that it's raining super hard.
Some idioms have meanings that are understandable by context ("You've got gossip about Nate? I'm all ears!"), and some have origins in stories and history (to "cry wolf" comes from one of Aesop's fables).
There are idioms in all languages. In fact, it's estimated that there are around 25,000 in the English language alone! Here are the idioms found in this book.
sitting duck: someone who is vulnerable to attack
big house: prison
rat race: a struggle for success, usually in business
a bull in a china shop: someone who is clumsy and reckless in a delicate situation
put the cart before the horse: to do things in the wrong order
you're canned!: you're fired!
beat it!: get out of here!
(more fun than) a barrel of monkeys: a whole bunch of fun!
a fish out of water: someone in an uncomfortable situation
red alert: a state of preparation for action
grab the bull by the horns: to deal with a problem confidently
on the case: doing what needs to be done

face the music: to accept the punishment you deserve
reap what you sow: accept the consequences of your actions
the price you have to pay: see above
on the double: quickly, now!
in a pickle: a difficult situation
water off a duck's back: something that has no effect
wrap it up: to stop what you're doing, to finish what you started
use your noodle: to think, to figure it out
dull as dishwater: extremely boring
barking up the wrong tree: making the wrong choice, the wrong assumption
pay an arm and a leg: to pay a lot of money
cook up: to plan, to scheme
cat got your tongue?: why aren't you talking?
hold your horses: wait, slow down
scapegoat: someone wrongly blamed
ELITE
TAXI SE
508-8
the chickens have come home to roost: something bad or foolish from the past has returned and is going to cause problems
something fishy (or "smells fishy"): something suspicious
monkey business: silliness, trickiness, or dishonesty
smell a rat: to suspect something is wrong
foul play: something illegal, dishonest, or unfair
no sweat: don't worry, no problem
don't count your chickens before they hatch: wait until what you're expecting to happen actually happens before moving forward
the sky's the limit: anything is possible!
a breeze: something easy
get your goat: usually means to annoy you, but Quentin uses it literally
k
stay tuned: we'll be back!

Amina's